# There's an 'F' in Phoenix

# in Redruth

## Les Merton

Published by Palores Publications 2007

There's an 'F' in Phoenix in Redruth
Copyright © Les Merton 2007

*Front Cover:*
Illustration and design Copyright © Trystan Mitchell 2007
*Back Cover:*
Photograph of Hayman House Copyright © Neil Williams
Photograph of Les Merton Copyright © Trystan Mitchell

ISBN 0-9551878-9-3
ISBN 978-0-9551878-9-6

*Published by:*
Palores Publications,
11a Penryn Street,
Redruth,
Cornwall.
TR15 2SP

*Designed and printed by:*
ImageSet,
63 Tehidy Road,
Camborne,
Cornwall.
TR10 8LJ

*Typeset in:*
Times New Roman 10pt
Stockton 15pt

There's an 'F' in Phoenix in Redruth

or

Theer's un 'F' en Feenix en Ridruth

Les Merton

# Acknowledgements

I would like to express a very special thank you to Trystan Mitchell (www.bigfootstudio.co.uk) for all the brilliant illustrations he has provided me with over the years; the staff at Kresenn Kernow, Redruth who are always there for me and to whom I am indebted for their time and knowledge, particularly on this occasion and I would like to credit Neil Williams for letting me use his photograph of the ruin of my former home, Hayman House taken on March 5th 2005, the day of the fire.

There are many prize winning stories and poems in this book: I do appreciate the judges of various competitions being so kind to me. Acknowledgement is also due to the magazines and books where some of this compilation first appeared. I'm sorry that I am unable to offer individual thanks - my records were destroyed by the fire.

Reliable printers are essential for all authors and I have a high regard for my printer, Mike Chapple of ImageSet. I would also like to mention how much I appreciated the help from Tony Lamb and Mick Paynter.

This book is also by way of a thank you to all those who helped me prove there is an 'F' in Phoenix in Redruth.

# Dedication

## To All Survivors

## *Author's Note*

I have tried to capture the sounds of Cornish dialect that I love and remember, by writing it phonetically. I believe this makes it easier for the reader and also, if read aloud, the words sound and feel authentic.

In the book words may occasionally be spelt differently to allow for variations of dialect in Cornwall.

It should also be noted that there are different ways of writing in dialect: some believe that speech alone should be rendered in dialect and the rest of the text in standard English; others write solely in dialect. The table of contents indicates which method I have used.

# Contents

## Stories

## Poetry

## Stories (including Cornish dialect)

## Poetry (including Cornish dialect)

## Stories (in Cornish dialect)

# Poetry (in Cornish dialect)

# The Ghost of Carndu

'... Which service do you require?'

'Police!'

'What is the nature of the incident?'

'I've just killed a man!'

'What is your name and address?'

'Tamsin Tregear. I live at Moor View Cottage at the foot of Carndu.'

'Stay where you are. The police will be with you shortly, Miss Tregear.'

'Please hurry...' Tamsin Tregear put the phone back gently onto its cradle, her upper lip trembled before she smugly smiled and hugged herself. Tamsin edged forward in the gloomy room and sat down in a chair near the window with heavy drawn curtains. She stretched out her hand, feeling blindly in the dark until she touched the cold barrels of the shotgun.

\*\*\*\*\*

Police Constable Cedric Thomas cursed the fog and cursed the fact that he had to cycle three miles from the village of Pencroft for the third time in as many days to Moor View Cottage.

\*\*\*\*\*

Tamsin Tregear slid her hand behind the curtain and slightly pulled it aside, she looked out into the pitch black of night. She smiled to herself when she saw the faint head light of a bicycle bobbing up and down as it slowly came closer.

\*\*\*\*\*

Cedric Thomas had been the police constable of Pencroft for the last 25 years. He loved his job and the hours of freedom it gave him to enjoy his large garden. The police constable made nearly as much selling vegetables to the villagers as he earned as a policeman.

Until this week, the only call out he'd had in the last six months was when Mrs Watson's cat was accused of killing one of Percy Moyle's budgerigars. This case was officially closed when the budgerigar in question was found alive and enjoying a spell of freedom in the church meadow.

Constable Thomas dismounted from his bicycle at the front gate to Moor

View Cottage garden. He moved his truncheon to a more comfortable position and considered how he should proceed. So far this week he had been called out to Moor View Cottage for a burglary where there was no sign of forced entry and nothing was taken. The next day he was called out again for an alleged attempted rape upon Tamsin Tregear. Both of the previous incidents had been in the daytime. This was a call-out at night and for a much more sinister reason.

Constable Cedric Thomas walked slowly up the garden path towards the cottage front door. He heard a noise and quickly turned around in the direction of the sound; switching on his torch as he did so. The beam from the torch revealed Tamsin Tregear standing by the side of the garden well.

Her long black hair masked her face, but didn't prevent Constable Thomas from seeing the obvious signal for silence as Tamsin raised a finger up to her lips. The police constable moved slowly towards her, she pointed down into the well and grabbed the water bucket from the ground and threw it over the parapet down into the well. Police Constable Thomas whipped out his truncheon instinctively at the sound of the roller on the well whirling around as the rope, attached to the descending bucket, unwound. A loud splash from deep below ground as the bucket hit the water underlined the sinister edge of night.

'I pushed him down into the well,' Tamsin exclaimed dramatically, pushing her hair back to reveal flashing wild eyes, she continued in a quick excited voice, 'and he went down faster than the bucket went down. He hit the water with a louder splash. I shouted to see if he was all right but he never answered. I know I killed him!'

'Killed who?' Police Constable Thomas asked, putting away his truncheon and flashing the beam from his torch down the well.

'The man who tried to rob me and I know now he was the same one that tried to rape me.' Tamsin answered in a positive tone.

'But who was it?' The constable asked impatiently.

'You know!' Tamsin Tregear shouted into Cedric Thomas's face.

'I don't!' The police officer retorted angrily.

'It was the ghost of Carndu.'

*****

Fire Officer Bill Williams pulled himself over the parapet of the well at Moor View Cottage. He signed, 'A trip for nothing Cedric, I don't really appreciate getting called out at first light to go down into the bowels of the earth looking for the body of a dead ghost.'

'I know!' Cedric grimaced, 'Tamsin Tregear has a lot to answer for!'

*****

The full cup of tea in a stained and chipped cup, with tea leaves floating on the top of it, was cold. Constable Thomas, pushed it to one side as he stood up.

'Thanks for the tea Miss Tregear, I'm sure you have nothing to worry about. I'll arrange for Doctor Pryer to call on you this morning.'

Tamsin Tregear stopped stroking the black motley cat on her lap, and pushed her hair back from her face. Her mouth twitched and her wild eyes flashed. In an abnormally quiet voice she said, 'I look forward to seeing Doctor Pryer again.'

*****

Emmanuel Pryer was a psychiatrist who worked with Cornwall Police. He was a tall, wiry man with a shaven head. His dark eyes seemed to look right through everyone he came into contact with. He parked his Ford Prefect in the lane outside of Moor View Cottage, picked up his small black bag, stepped out of the car and slowly walk up the path towards the front door. The cottage seemed deserted. He smiled as he remembered his last visit and wondered if Tamsin Tregear had any idea of what they'd done together when he had hypnotised her.

*****

Tamsin Tregear stood in the middle of the kitchen of her home facing the front door. Her eyes were used to the room's dark interior, the curtains were still drawn even though it was midday.

The knock on the door was loud and demanding. Tamsin pushed her hair away from her face, her mouth twitched before it formed a lopsided smile.

'Come in.' She commanded confidently and moved her feet slightly further apart to give herself a more solid stance.

Doctor Emmanuel Pryer opened the door and stepped into the room. He blinked to adjust his eyes to the dim interior now lit by a slither of light from the door he had just opened. Tamsin Tregear was standing in shadow, he could see the white outline of her body and realised she wasn't wearing any clothes . He took a pace towards her and stopped.

'Tamsin? Tamsin good to see you again.' He tried to sound positive although he felt a cold shiver down his spine.

He took another pace forward and saw Tamsin slowly raise her arms and point something at him.

'No! No don't Tamsin!' He screamed before the short range shotgun blast tore his body apart.

Tamsin didn't seemed to notice her body had been sprayed with blood from the man she had just shot. Her mouth twitched.

'That'll teach you to take advantage of me, when I trusted you to treat my depressions with hypnotism.'

She placed the shotgun on the floor beside the blood stained body, stepped back and hugged herself. 'When I have your child it will know its father's name lives on forever as the ghost of Carndu.'

# A MINER'S TALE

This story is based on fact, although some of the characters and incidents have been fictionalised.

John Pendrea, a Cornish tin miner, enjoyed the early morning September light on his walk across Carn Brea to work. Within minutes of his arrival, natural light would disappear and Dolcoath darkness would engulf him.

With the other miners on his shift, John Pendrea would descend to the depths of the *Queen* of Cornish mines, silently praying, as he always did at the start of each working day, for a safe return to the surface.

History left no Cornish miner with any illusions about the dangers associated with the job. Accidents and injuries, if not a daily occurrence, were at least a daily consideration.

The loss of twenty lives early that year, in the January of 1893, emphasised this region had a higher death rate than any other mining area in the country. In that incident, tons of water trapped in abandoned workings burst into the Wheal Oates mine in St Just. Nineteen men and a fourteen year old boy died.

Fatalities were regretted, families were consoled when they happened, but the impact of the tragedy was very short-lived. People involved in and around the mining community accepted the situation, and life moved on.

Across centuries, mining and religion walked hand in hand. St Piran, the patron saint of miners, as well as preaching to the locals, discovered tin when a black stone on his fire leaked a white liquid.

John Pendrea, like many other miners, rejoiced in the Methodist Hymn Book. He also had a deep belief in the power of the Bible to help him through the long and difficult times.

Another miner, Billy Bray, who died in 1868, became famous when he changed his drunken, swearing, life-style and accepted religion into his life. He went on to become an evangelist preacher. Although Billy worked down the mines for eight hours a day, he still had the energy and commitment to build several chapels.

Billy Bray's life-style had been an inspiration for John Pendrea. Even though he had no desire to preach, dance, or sing and shout the way the evangelist did, John Pendrea believed he felt the same inner warmth from his faith that Billy Bray had with his.

John Pendrea often said, 'My faith is deep and rich. It's fitting I work in the deepest, richest mine in Cornwall.'

On Tuesday 19th September 1893, Captain James Johns, Dolcoath's chief underground agent, and Captain Josiah Thomas, the mine manager, went almost half a mile underground to visit the 412 fathom level.

Captain Thomas knew that at some time the ground would have to be strengthened. Captain Johns reminded him that all that lay between the straining timbers and a mass of broken rock, was a thin layer of un-worked ground.

Both men were aware of the dangers of working at this level, and began their inspection of the 'stulls' (massive timbers placed at right-angles to the underside of the lode).

'Although I wouldn't be afraid to sleep here for twelve hours, I'm going to instruct John Pollard the chief timber man to strengthen this stull with two 20- inch timbers,' Captain Johns informed the mine manager.

\* \* \* \* \*

The next day, Wednesday 20th September, John Pendrea was one of a gang of workers in the 40 foot wide 412 fathom level. The morning work progressed well. In the early afternoon when one of the new timbers was ready to be put into place, there was a loud crack from one of the old stull timbers.

To the miners this warning was known as a *Godsend*. All the men started to run. Immediately the timbers gave way. John Pendrea, and seven other men working further back in the tunnel were trapped when, with a deafening roar, thousands of tons of rubble crashed down.

Only six miners, who were working at the level opening, reached safety. They shouted through clouds of dust. No sound came from their missing comrades.

\* \* \* \* \*

John Pendrea had no idea how long he was unconscious. Slowly, he came round to find himself in a small crevice between large boulders. Dust was still thick in the air. His body ached, but he realised the real agony came from his feet and legs trapped under a massive timber.

Slowly the dust settled, and gradually his breathing became easier. In the pitch blackness, John Pendrea closed his eyes to thank the Lord.

'John! John Pendrea, wake up! Tis me, Billy, come to keep you company.'

'Billy?' John tried to move. He gasped, as pain coursed through his body.

'Lay still John, help is on the way.'

John peered into the gloom. In the distance, he saw a wiry little man watching him, 'Who are you?' he asked.

'Tis me, Billy. Billy Bray! St Piran sent me to keep you company for a while.'

'Billy! What do you want me to do?'

Billy Bray smiled. 'Do? Why, do what we always do! Sing and pray of course, John! You must have heard the story of when I had ten men working down the mine with me. I used to pray for them in a simple language.'

John Pendrea nodded, and gasped again as pain racked through his legs.

'My Lord!' Billy Bray shouted, and continued in a lower tone, 'If any of us must be killed or die today, don't let it be one of these men. Let it be me. If I die today, I am ready to go to heaven.'

John Pendrea understood. The figure of Billy Bray faded, and John began to sing the hymns he knew and loved so well.

\* \* \* \* \*

At about 3 pm. on Thursday, over a day after the disaster had happened, a gang of men tunnelled in from the east side of the mine. They heard a voice cry out, 'Praise the Lord!'

Another hole was forced open between the rocks, and one of the rescuers was able to crawl to within twenty feet of John Pendrea.

'I can't get any nearer at the moment, but we'll do everything to get you out!'

'I'm easy,' John Pendrea replied. 'I can't move, my legs are trapped.'

'Anybody with you?'

'Just me and the Lord.'

Attempts to get food and drink to John Pendrea failed. Another tunnel was started in an attempt to get to him. Slowly the rescuers dug their way forward.

Word had spread like wildfire that one of the eight missing men was still alive. Even though it was pouring with rain, crowds of people from Camborne and the surrounding area gathered at the pit-top. News was slow in coming. Five hours passed before the first miner was rescued. Shortly afterwards, two other men were brought up to the surface. Both were dead.

The attempt to get the new tunnel through to John Pendrea seemed futile. As the hours passed, no cries for help were heard. The rescuers' efforts seemed to be in vain.

Tom Trewearne, known for his determination, was a veteran at mine rescue. He had worked with several other rescuers for hours, widening a narrow passage through the rubble. Huge bulks of timber surrounded by massive rocks were attacked with cross-saws. Eventually, the passage was opened enough to squeeze through.

Wriggling slowly forward, Tom Trewearne could only see a few inches in front of him. The light from his helmet candle continuously spluttered, threatening to go out. Although it was dangerous under such conditions, Tom's only thoughts were to get the poor men out, dead or alive.

He yelled, 'Can anyone hear me!'

'Down here, Billy.' A weak voice answered.

'Who is it?' Tom Trewearne asked.

'John Pendrea.'

Tommy Trewearne looked in the direction of the voice but could see nothing through the pitch black. 'Can you see my light, John?' he shouted.

'I can see the light. I'm making for the light, Billy!'

'It ain't Billy, it's Tom - Tom Trewearne! I must be only a few feet from you! I promise I'll get to you soon!'

Suddenly, everything went very quiet. Tom shouted. His own voice echoed back to him. He tried to edge his way forward, but once again, the passage became too narrow.

* * * * *

Almost two weeks after the disaster, on the 1st of October, Tom Trewearne, with other rescuers, finally reached John Pendrea. His feet were crushed. Death had evidently resulted from gangrene and a loss of blood.

Tom Trewearne said, 'I can't explain it, but I know John Pendrea didn't die alone. There was something, or somebody, down there with him. Somebody guiding him out of the darkness, to the light on a far horizon.'

# Barman's - Barman

Alfred is the barman's barman. He has class - real class, you wouldn't expect to find a guy of his like in this part of Cornwall, he would have been far better suited in the Cocktail Bar at The Ritz. Alfred talks softly in a posh accent and is very knowledgeable about world affairs; he could have had a private education or maybe went to Oxford or Cambridge he seems that type. Strange thing is, he never talks about himself and no-one has ever seen him with family or even any friends for that matter; come to think of it, Alfred never mentions his family or any of his friends in conversation.

Alfred is always clean shaven, his dark hair is short and neatly parted at the side. Someone once said, his large brown eyes reminded them of cow's eyes, they seem to have such an innocent, trusting quality. He always wears a clean white dress shirt and black bow tie, his black trousers have a sharp permanent crease and the matching shoes shine from regular spit and polish.

Alfred is amazing, he remembers everyone's name and preferences. He is very well mannered and discreet, never talks about his customers. The customers talked about him though: they say, he only works the local dive bars, because he has a past. The customers' whisper among themselves; did he rob the till in another establishment, perhaps in a more select neighbourhood. He could have had an affair with an employer's wife. Maybe he's gay and made a pass at a colleague or is he one of those that's done time for something more sinister.

All the regulars comment on how it's not natural for a man to be doing the job he's doing and not to have the odd tipple. Alfred only ever drinks coke from a tall, slim, chilled glass with a twist of lemon and a dice of ice. He works every day; morning, afternoon and evening shift until late. On the evening shift his large brown eyes seem to shade as he serves drink after drink to customers who have had too much and can hardly stand.

Recently Alfred has been taking Monday evenings off; he's very secretive about it. Although once he did let slip that it was to go to a meeting... . He said, more and more he feels the need to keep in touch.

# Palores

On a road leading from Boscastle to Tintagel, two large black birds were feeding. A slightly smaller bird with shiny, purple black plumage landed near them.

'What's your name?' Charlie the crow asked, before turning his attention to a morsel of discarded sandwich.

'I don't know.' The shy stranger replied, in a kee-ah tone. 'I don't know.'

Charlie cawed to his wife Charlotte, 'He's a stupid bird. Caw, he don't know his name. He can't be a crow, that's for sure.'

Charlotte preened a wing before answering her husband. 'He can't be a crow. Caw, his feathers are too shiny.
Caw, his feathers are too shiny.' (Charlotte always repeated herself.)

'He's a daw. Caw. Daws are black.' Charlie flew into a tree. Crows won't stand in the road if there's no food to be found. They don't like the man-made machines that run on roads. All crows know man-made machines are dangerous.

Charlotte joined Charlie on the branch. The shy stranger tapped the road with his beak and flew to a branch beside the crows. Mr and Mrs Crow looked at one another and then looked at their new companion.

'Caw, Caw.' Charlotte called Chas her son. Chas answered with a caw, before dropping from a higher branch to join them. 'Who's this?' Chas gestured with his beak towards the shy stranger.

'He don't know his name,' Charlie crow repeated for his son's benefit. 'Caw, I think he's a daw.'

'I'm not a daw! I do know my name. My name is Arthur! I've been away and I forgot that's all,' the stranger said dramatically.

'Another thing you forgot. Caw, the road is hard, you tapped your beak and now it's bent.' Charlotte said in a knowing, crowing way. 'Caw, you tapped your beak and bent it,' she emphasised.

'No I didn't, its always been this curved shape.' Arthur said defensively, looking down his nose at his beak, before wiping the red bill on a branch.

'Daws don't have curved bills,' Chas said, 'my best friend Dicky is a daw and he doesn't have a curved bill.'

'Caw. Daws' bills aren't red.' Charlotte bobbed her head to confirm what she had said, but decided that wasn't enough, so she repeated, 'daws' bills aren't red!'

'I'm not a daw. I'm palores.'

'Doesn't he talk funny, palores that's a foreign language word, my great,

great, great, grand father told me about a bird with the foreign language name palores.' Charlie exclaimed, twisting his head around to look over his shoulder. He was suddenly worried. Crows don't like talking about the past.

Charlotte turned her head, looked over one wing, then turned to look over the other. The only other birds to be seen were two magpies sitting on a gate in the distance. Crows are wary of magpies. Charlotte remembered human folklore, one for sorrow, two for joy.

The magpies were too far away to hear what she said. 'I remember my great, great, great, grandma saying, caw, crows had a distant cousin who had red legs. You've got red legs Arthur. Caw, are you a distant cousin?'. Charlotte paused. She could see Arthur was thinking. 'You've got red legs. Caw, are you a distant cousin?'

'I'm a member of the family Corvidae, that was one of my in-egg lessons. I remember now, we are cousins because you come from the same family.' Arthur felt pleased with himself, the fresh air is doing me good, he thought.

It was like lightning striking. The fresh air! It was only today he had really started to enjoy the fresh air. The memory floodgates burst open. It was just this morning that he had been released!

Arthur's mind raced, all of his family, his parents, his brothers and sisters were captive bred birds and he was the first of their kind to be returned to freedom. 'I'm a Cornish chough. I remember some of my in-egg history lessons. Man changed the way he farmed and this affected our feeding grounds. He also trapped us and sold us into slavery as pets. Hundreds of my kind died for nothing.'

'Yes, I remember that story too,' Chas interrupted. 'Caw, but you still have family in other countries, your bird family is not extinct like the dodo.'

'I know I have a mission!' Arthur declared, 'being captive bred has affected my memory. What is my mission?'

'Mission, caw, mission? Charlotte asked her husband.

Charlie looked up and down, looked left and right, then he whispered. 'Ask the wise old owl who lives in the man-made barn. Caw, he's not one of us, but caw, he comes from a good egg.'

'Caw.' 'Caw.' 'Caw.' The air was full of crow sounds and then there was silence. The Cornish chough was alone on the branch. Arthur pushed his memory way back to forgotten egg lessons.

He saw images of cliffs and sea, he flew on a flight of fantasy through caves, across rocks and water. He was free. This tree beside the road wasn't his home. Arthur smelled the air, the sea was near. He was about to fly towards the sea smell, when he remembered what the crows had said, 'Ask the wise old owl what your mission is.'

Instinctively Arthur felt afraid. He knew he wasn't a bird of the man-made barns. Something stirred inside him, commanded him to remember. It was as if he was inside the shell of his egg pecking his way out, slowly, because he was afraid. Suddenly, after another peck the fear vanished and he was outside of the shell.

Although Arthur wasn't a bird of the man-made barns, he would follow the crows' advice.

Flying inland for a chough is difficult. The sea always calls in its subconscious mind. Arthur blocked out the call of the sea. He flew inland across fields and pasture into the countryside until he saw man-made buildings.

One of the buildings had an opening near the top, and Arthur flew through it. A young female of the human species screamed. 'Get out of my bedroom.'

Arthur dipped a wing, swerved and flew outside again. Over the sound of his loudly beating heart, he heard a voice. 'Twit to woo, who are you, twit to woo.' Arthur knew instinctively it was an owl. He followed the sound through another opening into the man-made barn.

'I don't like being woken up at this time of day, you twit, twit to woo.' The voice was trying to be fierce, but the heart shaped face of the barn owl was so friendly that nothing except a mouse would have been frightened of it.

Arthur settled on top of a pitchfork and looked up at the barn owl perched above him on a cross beam. 'I have heard it said, that owls are very wise and can tell me what my mission is.'

The barn owl fluffed its feathers and closed one eye, 'That's known as folklore. I am no wiser than you.'

'What is folklore?' Arthur asked innocently.

'Folklore is what humans think about things they don't know about. Every bird has its own folklore. You should remember your folklore from your own in-egg lessons.'

'I can't remember. I am a captive-bred bird and I think it affected my vital in-egg lessons.

'A similar thing happened to my cousin, the eagle owl. He was bred from captive parents. His egg was put in an incubator to hatch. He suffered terrible memory problems because the egg sitting bonding from the natural parent was lost in his in-egg lessons,' the barn owl reflected sadly.

'Is there any cure?' Arthur asked. 'I want to know what my mission in life is.'

'There is only one cure if in-egg lessons fail. This cure is older than the human species, it's birds' natural instinct, known as the home to roost instinct.'

'I don't understand, please explain?' Arthur asked with interest.

'Since you have been free have you felt nature calling to you?'

'Before I came to see you, I smelled the sea and I wanted to fly to it.' Arthur replied.

'Go, go now, fly to the sea, I feel in my feathers you will discover what your mission is.'

Arthur flew out of the window, his senses directed him to the sea. He flew over the edge of the cliffs, he was so buoyant, he felt light headed.

Then a voice in an ancient language cried out from the sea below. 'Nuns nyns yu marow Myghtern Arthur.' The words echoed in the Cornish chough's memory and translated instinctively to, 'King Arthur is not dead.'

Arthur settled on the ramparts of a ruined castle. He was home at last. 'Kee-ha, kee-ha,' he called, 'I'm the spirit of a king. I know my mission!'

# Horlicks Memories

The following extracts have been taken from a Radio Kernow interview at Penfibber's Luxury Retirement Center.

He was as real as the chap next door and as British as fish and chips. Those were the days... .

Like many other famous people, of his generation, he looked for a slower pace of life. Somewhere to wind down. Although he had travelled extensively around the universe, there was only one place that he wanted to be... and that was Cornwall.

This is The Trelawney Programme and through the magic of Kernow Radio, here is another story of someone living near you in their own words...

\*\*\*\*\*

I've been down here for years. I consider myself a local. I even call it Kernow and I enjoy a pasty for crouste with the best of them. Do you know, I can't quite remember how long ago it was. But, I think. No, I'm sure... I used to be known as Dan Dare - pilot of the future.

If Miss Peabody, perhaps I should say Professor Jocelyn Peabody to acknowledge her properly... . No, Miss Peabody will do. Anyway Miss Peabody would have known how long I've been down here.

Miss Peabody, God bless her, she was a lovely girl.

Do you know? I never even kissed her, not even when we were marooned together on Mekonnia. Must say, damn fine girl Miss Peabody.

I no longer fly, of course. Well, not in the conventional way. I gave that up years ago, when I retired or got written out or something I don't remember. However, I do know it certainly wasn't that I got too old for the job. Got old, that's not true! I never got old.

I'm the same age now as I was then, if you know what I mean. I look the same, well not quite... . I don't wear that green uniform any more... these days I'm more casual: dressing gown, you know, the Marks and Spencer type, with down at the heel slippers to match.

I still look after myself of course. Well, you know, I look after, you know, the bits they can't do for you. Number ones and number twos - that type of thing. Still do that for myself. Chaps got to have his pride, you know.

One thing that never changes is Horlicks. Do you remember Horlicks?

Perhaps you don't, but I do. Every night on that Radio Luxembourg: 'Why is Dan Dare so fit and active?' You remember those lines don't you? 'Dan Dare is so fit and active because he drinks Horlicks.'

By gad, no one will ever know how much I hated the damn stuff and I still do! Now, they feed it to me intravenously. Do you know, even the Mekon wasn't capable of a diabolical trick like that. He wasn't that cruel...

You know, I haven't seen him for years. Funny chap, green all over. Well, we assume he was green all over. Never did see the little chap without his uniform.

Not like you know... . No! No, not Miss Peabody. Not Professor Peabody, never even kissed her, you know. Not even when we were marooned on Mekonnia.

Sorry about that, the old space ship got a bit diverted. Hot air currents does things to a chap. You know I never even kissed Miss Peabody... .

Now where was I. Ah yes! The Mekon, he was a very funny little chap, never walked anywhere. He used to float around on that little dish. Do you remember? The little green Mekon floating around on that dish. My gad, those where the days, still are of course.

We never nailed that little green chap. I still have nightmares wondering what he's up to. Must say the Horlicks does help. Two cups full and I'm gone, amazing stuff Horlicks. You know although the Mekon was a diabolical chap, he never took advantage of me when I was zonked out on Horlicks. I said to myself. 'Gosh Dan, you know, he can't be that bad after all.'

Now, I can admit it, I had a soft spot for that little chap. I never let on of course, wouldn't have done... . Me, a high ranking officer in the Interplanetary Space Fleet, having a soft spot for one of our enemies. I blame the loneliness of space , you know, it does things to a chap. All that space... all that space.

Never even kissed her you know... . By gad, Miss Peabody looked good in that uniform, green suited her.

Miss Peabody said to me once. 'Dan, I'm so proud of my uniform, I never wear any knickers underneath. Just in case the outline of the knickers shows through and spoils the figure hugging cut of the uniform.'

Damn fine girl Miss Peabody... . Never even kissed her, you know... . Digby will back me on that one.

Yes Digby, you must remember Digby. Albert Fitzwilliam Digby, sometimes affectionately called Dig. Digby and me were very close. Doesn't pay to talk about, respect for the uniform and all that. One thing I can say about Digby - fine chap. Damn fine chap.

You know, I never even kissed Miss Peabody. I never once kissed dear Professor Peabody, even though she looked lovely in the green figure hugging uniform. She never used to wear any knickers you know, didn't want to spoil the cut of the uniform.

Now were was I? Ah, yes Digby. Damn fine chap Digby. He always looked dignified in that green uniform. Although he did wear knickers.... . Double stitched Y fronts I seemed to remember.

He always looked good. Yes, Digby always look good.

If you remember, I couldn't say if the Mekon was green all over. Digby would agree with me on that, we never did see the Mekon out of his uniform.

Come to that, we never saw Miss Peabody out of her uniform either. But, I'm sure Miss Peabody would be a lovely cream colour all over. She would have wanted to look right underneath her uniform, especially without any knickers on.... .

I never even kissed her, you know. Digby will vouch for that.

Dear old Digby, with that white hair and that lovely soft skin. Digby was a fine upstanding chap. Ah, dear old Digby... he was lovely in every way.

I said to him once. 'Dig, old chap, if I didn't have you... I might have kissed Miss Peabody.'

# Widower
*(based on a true incident)*

Everyday since his retirement, Bert had watched his wife Mary's daily routine from the comfort of his armchair. She would give a gentle flick with her feather duster over ornaments bought as presents by long forgotten friends. Everyday she would wipe the only ashtray with a yellow duster, just in case a guest, who she couldn't recall calling, ignored the no smoking signs. Mary's straightening of the crotched chair covers was done with tender love; out of respect for former deft fingers and a mind that believed the personal touch made a home.

As well as Mary's daily formalities, there was her weekly ritual; whatever the weather, day in day out she kept to it. Monday - washday, Tuesday - Women's Institute, Wednesday - hoovering, Thursday - shopping, Friday - baking, Saturday - bingo, Sunday - roast lunch and evening church service.

Suddenly everything changed. Mary never said she was going. Bert can still remember being woke up from his mid-morning nap in the armchair. He never understood why, but it stuck in his mind: this was the terrible day they made him dress in his black ill-fitting suit, white shirt, black tie and polished shoes instead of his favourite down at the heel slippers.

The church was a very sad place, full of half-remembered people who sang hymns from another time. Bert remembered crying when he walked behind the coffin. It had started to rain by the time they reached the open grave. Bert wanted to go home and sit in his armchair by the cheerful coal fire, but they kept him there standing in the rain. A man with a funny white collar held an umbrella to shelter him, while everyone filed past and shook his hand; they all said similar things to him. Bert didn't understand why they were all so sorry. He stopped listening after a while.

However, it did get better; there was the ride in the big black car to a strange house; everyone was given a cup of hot tea - his had loads of sugar in it. Best of all was the ham sandwiches. He enjoyed ham sandwiches; Mary in fifty years of being married to him never bought ham, simply because she didn't like it.

After that Bert's memory seemed to blur: he kept sleeping and waking up in the armchair. And sleeping and waking up in the bed. And sleeping and waking up in the armchair...

Until he remembered what his wife Mary used to say to him everyday; 'You'll die in that armchair. You will Bert, you'll die in that armchair!'

He'd show her... the old fuss pot.

From that moment, Bert made up his mind to fill his days in the very same way his wife Mary used to do. He started straight away: the ornaments were easily knocked off shelves with a heavy-handed flick of a feather duster; still, it made less work, he told himself. To save dusting the ashtray he put it the cupboard out of site, that way no-one who smoked would leave ash in it. Crotched chair covers stained easily with dirty hands, best leave them crumpled, what did it matter. His activities and resourcefulness made him feel there was still a reason for living.

This was enhanced by his new weekly ritual; Bert wasn't sure of the days, but that didn't really matter; he'd have a go at hoovering and washing; no point in baking, some woman with a uniform always left cooked food and the occasional cake, plus if he remembered to ask her nicely, by saying please, she would make him ham sandwiches. Bert decided against the library, he wasn't fond of reading. The widower quickly got into the routine of them collecting him for bingo and on Sundays he went out with them to a hall with a lot of really old people, (he felt a bit out of it as they were all so old. Nevertheless Bert enjoyed the roast lunch and afterwards put on a brave face to go to the evening church service.

Bert never did go to the Women's Institute, although once a week he'd dress especially. He'd put on her flowery frock and navy hat with a peacock feather. Mary always liked to look smart for her Tuesday outing.

# ootball Mad

ommy Lugg was football mad. Before Tommy could walk his father Percy sed to take him by train every other Saturday to watch Plymouth Argyle's ame at Home Park, on the alternate weeks they use to watch one of the ocal Cornish village sides play.

Even before he went to school Tommy made up his mind that when he rew up he would be a professional footballer playing for Plymouth Argyle. lthough it might seem character-building for someone as young as Tommy ) have such a noble ambition, in reality it was all rather sad.

Life being what it is Tommy's football career would be an uphill struggle s well as a non-starter. Tommy didn't have a clue about how to play football. Ie had two left feet and neither of them was attached to his brain.

Unaware of the cruel comments about him, at eight years old Tommy ccidcd to join in and play football with the older boys at school. He pproached both teams and said he didn't mind which position he played in s long as he could join in the game. Unfortunately both teams had prior nowledge of Tommy's soccer ability and rejected him.

Undeterred, Tommy watched from the sidelines. Every day he would sk if he could join in with that day's game in the school playground. The nswer was always no, although eventually he was allowed to be a goal ost.

After a few days of standing as straight as he could Tommy began to magine himself above his station. Depending on the state of play, he would e either a referee or a coach in his own mind.

Unfortunately, as a coach Tommy's comments were totally ignored. Iowever, one day the goal-post in his alter-ego as a referee, spotted a foul nd shouted, 'Hand ball!'

It was hotly disputed by the offending player and his team-mates, but ustice prevailed. There would be a penalty. Before it could be taken the enalty spot was disputed and Tommy being neutral was asked to pace it ut.

Tommy took the biggest twelve strides he could and declared where he hought the penalty spot should be. Unfortunately Tommy was rather short nd his twelve paces were only six yards form the goal line.

Returning to his normal role as a goal post, Tommy watched the biggest oy in the school, known by one and all as Snowy on account of his always iaving a drop at the end of his nose (like snow dripping off a roof.)

Snowy walked the length of the pitch before he started his run to take the penalty. Tommy watched Snowy thunder down the field. He really booted the ball; it shot off like a rocket and hit Tommy full in the face and made his nose bleed.

'Hard luck Snowy, you hit the goal post!' his team mates shouted.

# Let's Experience Cornwall

Let's catch the light down in St Ives,
Rock Logan Stone upon its perch,
Kneel at the grave where Jenner lies,
And find peace in Gunwalloe Church.

Let's see the magic in Merlin's spells,
Lament for Tristan and Iseult at Castle Dore,
Hear the ghostly sounds of Lyonesse Bells
And climb Brown Willy and Roughtor.

Let's show our pride on St Piran's Day,
Leave footprints in the sand at Gyllingvase,
Light a Midsummer Eve's bonfire on Carn Brea,
And sing a Gwennap Pit song of praise.

Let's believe in healing power at Holywell,
Acknowledge our coasts' potential to wreck,
Admire the edifice of Roche Rock's Chapel
And celebrate harvest with *crying the neck.*

Let's watch the cascade at Golitha Falls,
Explore below grass down in Geevor mine,
Listen in awe as King Arthur's spirit calls
And touch the polished face of serpentine.

Let's follow paths lined with golden gorse,
Collect shells on the beach at Porthcurnow,
Go from Troy Town to its river's source
And rest in Hawker's hut at Morwenstow.

Let's honour this experience at the close,
Help our culture and history to survive,
Respect Cornwall in its metamorphose
And enjoy the quintessence that's alive.

# Outhouse

The outhouse door was closed,
behind it, everything a boy
needed for a summer day.

His cricket bat, with a history
of sixes through windows,
a real cricket ball, no longer red,
its split seam perfecting spinners.

The outhouse door wasn't locked,
nobody even locked their front doors,
you could trust your neighbours.

Nothing living like rats
or dead like a stuffed raven
nor in between like bogey men
kept a boy from the outhouse.

The outhouse door never moved,
no matter how the adder thrashed
the nail that secured it held.

When its poison drained
the snake died, the nail remained,
its height ideal for a boy to hang
his dart board on summer nights.

# n the presence of a standing stone

As maidens they cast pins and needles
into the water of a holy well to discover
their fate in the brightness of bubbles.

Now in the presence of a standing stone
they reminisce - memories blur time,
myth, magic and spirit of place into one.

The tranquillity of clay mountains
are a perfect back-drop for the sound
of Corn Gwlas and the cry for peace.

St Michael's Chapel frame growing
romantically out of the Rock
is a pivot for imagination.

Its cell was the hermitage of a leper
who was tended to by his daughter,
Gundred, with daily food and water.

Tregeagle, giant of myth, howled
for sanctuary at the chapel window
when pursued by Devil's hounds.

In summer there were picnics out Rock
when you could watch our choughs
and be uplifted by the spirit of Arthur.

And the children couldn't get enough
of mopp-and-hideaway among boulders
in a park that twins fantasy and nature.

# Medlyn Moors

The paths leading to a knacked bal
are those walked long ago by men
from Viscar, Porkellis, Halwin,
Polhigey, Carnkie and Halabezack.

These men were tin miners
who had no illusions about the hazards
they faced working the sett, below grass
to eke out a meagre living.

I knew every path that crossed the moor
and traversed them all at different times
as Geronimo, Ghengis Khan, Robin Hood,
Kit Carson and even as Fabian of The Yard.

I was never a tin miner;
but, I had no illusions about the hazards
I faced fighting and winning battles:
Dunkirk, Waterloo, Little Big Horn.

Had I known about Michael Joseph An Gof
and Thomas Flamank, I'd have fought and won
the Battle of Blackheath on Medlyn Moors
time and time again.

# Dozmary Pool

Water as solemn
as depths of loneliness,

immersed in mysteries
of days long gone,

reflecting clouds of despair,
deliberating on desolation.

Century after century,
mesmerised by belief:

a sword shining
below surface

confirms legend,
justifies faith.

# A Day in the Life of Ivor Denbal

'Woss on en me ansum?''

Ivor Denbal stopped straining and looked in the direction of the voice. It belonged to Constable John Pascoe, known locally as Long John on account of the underwear he wore unofficially under his police uniform. The very same underwear his wife advertised, as a true example of police whiter than white, every Monday on her washing line, outside the police house, in Penfibber.

'Nawthun.' Ivor Denbal replied, standing up straight in the dustbin. Long John took out his notebook, looked at his watch, licked his pencil, and started to recite as he wrote. 'On Friday, the first of April, at 11a.m. whilst patrolling the lane that runs west of the post office in Penfibber, I saw a person know to me as Ivor Denbal standing in a dustbin. He was straining at the dustbin handles. When asked what he was doing. He said, 'Nawthun', in a dialect that confirmed he was a resident from the bottom end of the village.'

Police Constable Long John Pascoe, licked his lips and dropped his official Police English. 'I sid woss on? Yewr standun en thet dustbin lik tha village idiot. Naw, I didun mane thet. Wen thay sent yew ome, fram St Lawrences, yew ad a certificaate ta saay yew waas sane.'

As if that was his cue, Ivor Denbal gripped the dustbin handles and started to strain. His face went bright red with the effort. He let go the dustbin handles and let out a long sigh.

'Tis naw gud Long John, I mane Mistar, I mane Constable Pascoe.'

Thinking this could be a break through in crime detection, Long John Pascoe licked his pencil and said, 'Come on son you can tell me all about it, why don't you step out of that dustbin and come for a cup of suggery tea down at the nice, very nice, police house.'

'Caan't.'

'Wat doee mane... What do you mean young man?' Constable Pascoe asked with true police efficiency.

'Caan't.'

'Don't caan't me!' Long John exclaimed and gave Ivor a quick clip under the ear.

'Yew caan't et me en tha chacks. I'll ave tha law un yew!' Ivor shouted.

'I am tha law you saffron bun short of a tea-treat!' Police Constable Pascoe snapped. He sneered, 'I'm arresting you for being a public nuisance.'

'Caan't.'

'Can.' Replied Long John, getting out his handcuffs.

'Caan't!' Ivor repeated, gripping the dustbin handles and straining upwards again. 'I'm trainun, I am, I'm trainun.'

'Trainun?'' Asked the bewildered policeman, 'Training? Training, what re you training for?' Long John held up his hand for silence. This, by the way, is the same signal as the prescribed signal, police use to indicate motorist to stop. He put his handcuffs away and proceeded to bring his otes up to date. He narrated, 'I asked the person known to me, as Ivor Denbal, what he was training for?'

Police Constable Pascoe smiled the smile he always smiled when the udge said, 'Take him down, officer.'

'Training?' The Police Officer cross-examined cunningly.

'Trainun. Trainun ta bay a wraslar!'

'What!'

'I'm trainun ta bay a wraslar!'

Long John paused; the cogs of police methods of interrogation slipped n to gear. He asked in procedure mode, 'All In Wrestling or Cornish Wrestling?'

'Boath.' Ivor replied with a smile, that didn't make him look quite fitty, ollowed by a grunt as he strained at the dustbin handles.

'Please explain in full detail.'

'Wraslars ave gotta bay strong ta lift tha othur bloke. Percy tha Poastman id, ta bay a wraslar, I ad ta bay strong nuff ta lift myself up whilst I waas tandun en a dustbin.'

Police Constable John Pascoe drew himself up to his full height, (one undredth of a inch below the minimum police regulation height, he had tuck hairs to the soles of his feet for his police entrance examination and ot in by a whisker.) 'Ivor Denbal I'm arresting you on suspicion of wasting olice time. I must remind you anything you say may be taken down in writing and used as evidence against you in a court of law. Do you understand?'

Ivor Denbal's mouth went abroad like a fish out of water. He nodded.

'Good!' Long John put away his note book and pencil and pulled out his olice whistle. He made a long exaggerated attempt to blow it. Not a single ote came out.

John Pascoe took the police whistle out of his mouth and held it up to he light. He shook his head in dismay. Ivor watched in silence, his curiosity rowing by the minute.

'The reason I tried to blow my police whistle is, I need help to take you and the evidence,' he pointed to the dustbin, 'down to the police station. However the pea seems to have fallen out of my whistle. Seeing I can't summon any of the afore said help.' Police Constable Long John, Pascoe paused for a dramatic effect, (for a definition of dramatic effect see Police procedure, chapter 2, paragraph 3), 'I'll tell you what I'm prepared to do.'

Ivor nodded, listening intently.

'I want you to get out of the dustbin, go down to the village and ask Percy the Postman, if I can borrow the spare pea he has got for his whistle and bring it back here to me. If you do this... I'll ask the judge to take it easy on you in court.'

Ivor stepped out of the dustbin and ran like a long dog towards Percy the Postman's house. Police Constable Long John, Pascoe took his notebook out of his pocket, tore out the recently written pages and threw them in the dustbin.

# The Romans Come to Cornwall

Once upon a time, the Roman army came to invade Cornwall. They had heard what a good place it was for pasties, clotted cream, pilchards and tin, and the local maids weren't too bad either.

The Romans crossed the Tamar in the middle of the night in the hope of creeping up on the sleeping Cornish and taking them by surprise. As they walked down the A30 on tiptoe whispering 'Sssh!' to each other, a voice pierced the darkness ahead of them.

'Woss on me Ansums?'

The Legionnaire in charge muttered, 'Drat!' under his breath and then shouted towards the distant gloom, 'Now look here my good man, we've come to invade you and do the odd bit of pillage. If you'll put your hands up, and come quietly, we'll go easy on you.'

'Wull,' said the Cornish voice, 'Cud ycw cum back dreckly, as I'm ere on my own 'n' I'm atin' me pasty - 'tis crouse time, naw wat I mane do-ee.'

'No, you put your hands up and stand aside and we won't harm you,' said the Legionnaire getting really agitated - he could smell the pasty.

'I'll tellee wat,' suggested the voice from the gloom, 'yew send yewr bess man ovur, yew knaw, yewr best fightur, an ef ee bates me, then I'll let yew pass. '

The Legionnaire laughed, 'Ha! ha!' He called for Brutus Maximus, a mountain of a man, armour-plated from head to foot. A mighty shield in one hand, and a fearsomely sharp sword in the other.

'Go and sort him out,' commanded the Legionnaire.

Brutus Maximus disappeared into the darkness. Moments later loud crashes and bangs were heard, followed by a muffled scream and a dull thud. Suddenly the large shield of Brutus Maximus came flying through the air to land at the feet of the Legionnaire.

'Wan up ta me!' the Cornish voice taunted. 'Es thet tha best yew caan do? Send ovur yewr ten top fighters. I kin take em on an stull ate me pasty!'

Ten evil looking men, armed to the teeth, marched abreast into the darkness. There were more loud crashes and bangs, followed by screams, huds and then silence. From out of the darkness came the familiar voice, Nixt!'

The Legionnaire became worried about his reputation. He ordered a hundred men to charge into the blackness. The angry heavily armed men ran down the road and disappeared into the darkness. The familiar crashes, bangs and screams filled the air.

After a few moments of silence, the voice called out, 'Geve me a moment ta roll ma sleeves up... . Right, ready wen yew ar me Ansums.'

The Legionnaire divided up the remaining men into threes, 'You take the left, you the right, and the rest straight ahead.'

The Romans charged forward, axes, swords, knives, spears held aloft and shouting blood curdling cries they disappeared into the night. The sounds of fighting went on for over ten minutes. Crashes, thuds, screams and bangs then silence. Out of the blackness appeared a Roman soldier, covered in blood. Slowly, he staggered back along the road to collapse at the Legionnaire's feet.

'What happened?' demanded the Legionnaire.

'It's a trick,' replied the soldier, 'there's two of them!'

# Three Pints a Night

Gordy Ferguson bought The Wreckers pub so he could live in a village, by the sea, in his favourite part of the world Cornwall. Gordy, like many others before him tried to be accepted from the start. On his first night, as landlord of The Wreckers, Gordy gave out free beer to all the local customers... .

'Thus es propur,' Courtney Penaluna said in a dialect befitting a man from Porthtwuddentall, 'Corse et wud be bettar ef yew cud understan wat thet up tha countray fellow es un bout.'

'Iss, I've nawtess thet bra many ov em for-in-ners doan't talk fitty.' Sammy the Ferret added.

At the end of Gordy's first night at The Wreckers everyone was in a good mood. Gordy already knew the difference between beer and bitter and felt he was a local already.

Over the next few days Gordy tried to get involved in every way that he could. The lunch time tradition in The Wreckers was for the fisherman and other locals who came in to have a game of euchre with their pasty and pints. Gordy asked to be dealt in. After having the rules explain, Gordy was dealt five cards in the normal fashion of twice around the table by the dealer. Gordy did get to look at his cards but that was all...

Every game Gordy's partner Dewey Pascoe said the same thing. 'Dip yew partner, I'm playun a lone and.'

Give Gordy his due, he did play by the rules and thraw his hand in every time. When Dewey Pascoe euchred his rivels, Nobby Bolitho, one of his opponents said,'Yew waas sittun tightur then a gin, Dewey.'

Thinking a drink had been ordered, Gordy crossed to the bar and brought back a straight gin for Dewey who said, 'Propur job, nothun lik a partner who treets ee wan yew win a and!'

Knowing he had been had, Gordy left the locals to it and went to ponder on the last question made to him by Wally Jenkin, 'Can ee fathom thus wan owt Gordy, ef yew got Benny, Right, left en yer and can ee stull be beat?'

Gordy never did fathom out the euchre question, but over the next two weeks Gordy got to know his regular customers and more important he began to understand them.

One evening just as he was about to ring the bell for last orders; a man on his own and unknown to Gordy walked into The Wreckers. The new arrival ordered three pints of beer. Gordy hesitated but he thought, serve the man. Gordy placed the three pints in front of the customer and took his money. The customer down the three pints one after the other and left the bar immediately.

From that night on the new customer came into the pub just before the last orders bell, bought himself three pints and drunk them straight down and left immediately.

Gordy asked his regulars about the man and was told, 'Thet's Jan Lugg, ee liks ta keep imself to imself so we let im git un weth et.' Every time Gordy asked he got much the same answer. He wanted to know more. It was difficult to get into conversation with Jan, especially seeing how fast he drank his beer.

As quickly as Jan Lugg had appeared on the scene, he suddenly stopped coming into the pub. Again Gordy asked his regulars what at happen to the three pints a night man. The explain, that Jan had been coming to The Wreckers for a month, now he would support the nearby Fisherman's Arms for a month then come back to The Wreckers again.

Sure enough as soon as a month had past Jan Lugg entered The Wreckers at an earlier time of 10 o'clock, but the earlier time wasn't the only change. He went straight up to the bar and ordered two pints of beer instead of three. Gordy was puzzled but said nothing, he would ask his regulars tomorrow the reason for the change in Jan's drinking habits. However another puzzling change followed: instead of drinking the two pints straight down, Jan took them over to a table in the corner, sat down in an old rocking chair and took his time drinking them.

Gordy question his regulars the reason for the change and got a stock answer, 'Thas Jan Lugg yew, ee liks ta keep imself to imself so we let im git un weth et.'

Gordy had to find out, one night when it was quiet, and Jan Lugg was settled into the rocking chair sipping his first pint, Gordy edge across to him.

'Enjoying your pint Mr Lugg?' The landlord asked with a smile.

Jan Lugg glanced up at his host and took another sip of beer rather than answer.

Before Gordy could ask another question, Courtney Penaluna shouted across from the bar, 'Nother wan ef yew plaise landlord.'

When Gordy had served his customer he noticed Jan Lugg had drunk his beer and left.

The next night, Gordy had a plan. As soon as Jan Lugg ordered his beer his host said, 'Go and sit down in the rocker Mr Lugg, I'll take these across to your table.'

Jan Lugg looked like he was going to object, he paused, glanced left and right, clenched and unclenched his fist. Then he shrugged and sauntered over to the table where Gordy had set his pints. Jan picked up a pint and took a sip while standing.

Gordy, hovering on the other side of the table, said, 'It's a good pint tonight, see how creamy the head is. Sit down and enjoy it, Mr Lugg.'

Jan Lugg stared at Gordy, before raising the glass to his lips and gulping the rest of the pint down in one swallow. He placed the empty glass on the table and picked up the second pint and walked back to the bar with it.

Gordy hesitated, then he picked up the glass Jan had just emptied and gather up a couple of other empty glasses before going back behind the bar. Jan looked at Gordy and sauntered back across the room with his full pint which he set down on the table before sitting in the rocking chair.

Before Gordy could make up his mind what to do next, Sammy the Ferret put his empty pint glass on the bar and said, 'Ee liks ta keep imself to imself, does Jan, nothar beer ef yew plaise me Ansum.'

Gordy pulled Sammy the Ferret's pint and put it in front of him. Gordy asked, 'Why does he like to keep himself to himself?'

'Thas tha waay Jan es, ee liks ta keep imself to imself,' and with that Sammy the Ferret went back to his seat to watch the dart players.

The next night brought torrential rain and The Wreckers had few customers. Just before 10 p.m. Jan Lugg came in looking like a drowned rat. Gordy offered him a towel to dry his face and hair while he poured the customary two pints.

Jan looked at Gordy, took a sip from one of his pints before handing the wet towel back to Gordy.

'Thenks me Ansum, et's bucketun down owt theer, I waas gwain ta go ʈn Tha Fishermans wheech es nearer ta ome; but I thawt, naw stick ta me ᵓlan ta be feer ta both pubs en tha village.' Jan stated with a smile.

Gordy smiled, 'It's appreciated.'

'Yewr not fram roun ere ar ee?' Jan asked.

'No I'm from up north!' Gordy replied.

'Es I kin tull thet, yew doan't tawk fitty do ee.'

Gordy smiled, 'But I can understand all my customers now, but I must admit, it was hard work at first.'

'Iss spose. With that Jan picked up his two pints and walked across to is normal table and chair.

Gordy waited until there was only Jan and himself left in the bar. He walked across and sat down in the chair opposite Jan.

'Thought I'd join you for a minute,' Gordy said.

Jan stared at his full pint before looking up and nodding.

'Can I buy you a pint?' The landlord ventured.

Jan shifted uneasily in his chair, 'Naw,' he said, 'I onlay ave toe pints a nite.'

'I can remember when you used to have three pints a night.' Gordy replied with a smile, that would have made the publicans night class teacher proud.

'Iss thas rite.' Jan admitted and glanced around the bar. Even though there was no one else in The Wreckers he beckoned Gordy to come closer with his finger.

Gordy leaned across the table, 'And?'

Jan lower his voice to a whisper, 'Thas rite, I use ta ave thray pints a nite, wan fur me brothur up en Lanson, wan fur me othur brothur ovur Trura n wan fur me self.' Jan sighed and sat back in the chair.

Gordy nodded, 'You used to drink their health?'

'Iss, yew cud saay thet.'

Gordy felt uneasy but he had to ask, 'As something happened to one of your brothers with you now only having two pints a night.'

Gordy held his breath it seemed ages before Jan shifted in his chair and leaned forward. Jan glanced around the room and beckon with his finger once again. Gordy leaned across the table. This time Jan spoke directly into Gordy's ear in a whisper.

'Naw, me brothurs es oall rite, ef yew must naw, I've stopped drinkun me self, I jus ave the toe pints ta ave a drenk fer me brothurs.'

# Viscar Cottage

Does aura of my birth linger
in cob walls of Viscar Cottage?

Is there memory of midwife,
traces of father's pacing
or mother's pain and joy?

Did ancestral spirits
discuss my birth in Kemewek?
'Map aral rak Kernow.' *

Was the continuing lineage of
Merton, Hosking, Lander, Pascoe
celebrated with Celtic blessing?

The family skeleton
in the spence would have been
aired with dialect familiarity,

'Twudden Bessie's fault,
sha waas jus tha kitchun maid
do-un wat sha waas tolt ta do.
Ee tuke advan-taage over.

Would the baby be effected
by past misdemeanour? 'Wull
non ov es famlay waas - tis
waatur undur tha bridge.

Did they praise the Lord, sing hymns
and pray for me in Edgecumbe Chapel?
Did an uncle or a cousin buy a pint
in Halfway House to wet my baby head?

If I go back to Viscar Cottage today
will the ambience of birth open doors
for a journey beyond mother's womb
to my place within the Nation?

*another son for Cornwall

# Desmond

never played football
on school playground tarmac
with the boys,

or ran races trying
to beat the Sou' west wind
with his class mates.

He held court,
sat on the only dustbin
in the school yard,
going on and on
about his bus conductor ambition.

Desmond knew every bus stop
on the three different routes
between Falmouth and Penzance.
He could quote fares, time tables,
regulations, bus and route numbers.

After school, Desmond changed
into a bus conductor's uniform
to punch his ticket collection.

At weekends he built buses
from Meccano sets with lights and bells
that worked and a mirror on the stairs
to check the upper deck.

School Sports Days
were different. Teachers
made Desmond enter every race.
He ran like a long dog winning easily.

Desmond could have beat
the Sou' west wind, instead
when he left school he made the buses run to time.

# Fish into Rock

(1)
The huer watches from the cliff top.
He can spot change - red, purple, silver moving,
staining water- a shoal of pilchards playing the surface.

A bray of horns and ancient language
lives through the huer's trumpet.
                    *Hevva! Hevva! Hevva!*

Fishermen take up the cry
running through narrow streets.
                    *Hevva! Hevva! Hevva!*

Dogs bark, women shout,
children shriek, excitement echoes.
                    *Hevva! Hevva! Hevva!*

2)
The huer signals:
calico covered bushes moving
like synchronised Turk's heads pass
on time honoured semaphore instructions.

In the stem, seine boat and follower wait.
Eye and action follow the huer's gestures.
Weigh anchor. Go out to sea.

Shouts echo from the huer's trumpet.
                    *Get all ready! Get all ready!*
Bushes are brought down once
                    *swung around backwards - steady, steady...*

Cowl Rooz! Cowl Rooz! Cowl Rooz!

Seine nets are cast. The pilchards
are just like sheep herded into a pen.
Net ends are tacked - the door is closed.
The fish are incarcerated in a twine prison.

(3)
Gulls scream and plummet
over secured seine nets
as tucking begins:

*What do you say boys?*
*All together! Now, now, now!*
*Up, up, up she comes!*

Wicker baskets dip
pilchards from the sea, tip
liquid silver streams

into waiting boats:
laden to the gunwales
they head for harbour.

(4)
The landed catch is loaded into gurries
with a man at either end. They hurry

through winding streets watching for children
cabing fish as they pass. On to the fish cellar.

Drop off the pilchards: back again to the harbour,
a perpetual succession empty gurries - full gurries.

(5)
Inside the fish cellar, there's noise and confusion.
Every type of female: old crones to young maids:

ugly, sweet, lean, bad-tempered, mean
a congregation of the fair sex

working, talking, joking, squabbling, singing,
lamenting, shrieking, shouting, screaming,

*more fish, more salt, more fish, more salt.*
*a bucket of fish, a bucket of salt,*

A floor area is swept clean.
A layer of salt put down,

hands move as fast as tongues;
a layer of fish, a layer of salt -

smooth out fine:
bulking fish, bulking the fish,

a layer of fish, a layer of salt-
smooth out fine - time after time;

layer after layer - bulking the fish,
to the required height.

(6)
Four or five weeks pass; fish sufficiently
cured are broken out from the bulk, washed
and placed in hogsheads by fish maidens;

tails to the center - full barrels are capped
with a buckler - ready for pressing
out the oil before exporting the fish.

(7)
*Betwixt the two poles*
*there is nothing like pilchards*
*for saving of souls.*


*Author's notes:*

Title: *Fish into Rock* from the old Cornish saying, *Corn up in shock.*
*Fish into rock.*

*Betwixt the two poles/there is nothing like pilchards/for saving of souls.*
The adoption of the Christian faith with abstinence from eating flesh at
certain times and the reliance of fish is commemorated by this old rhyme in
St Ives.

# Ambis-shun

'Yew daun't knaw nawthen. En yew aint got naw ambis-shun.' Tha Tacher's words rung en Young Wullie's ears as ee trapsed ome fram skool. Tha en et term raa-port, stuff'd en es trousies pawkut, waas tha salt un tha wound ef an oall red-dee caaned back-side.

Mawthur un a pinny, thet sha ad wash'd tha collur owt ov, waas en tha kitchun cook'n raw fry. Faathur waas buzzy maakun rollies, an tell un Mawthur bout, nother furse fire. Faathur blam'd tha emmets fer smokin custum maade fags, ee expla-aned. 'Thay oall ad gov-ment pawder en em, ta make em burn fastur, an didun go owt whan yew ditch em.'

Young Wullie cam ome fram sko-ool, sat down en tha harm cheer by tha Cornish Range. Mawthur commented, 'Yer braa an quate Young Wullie, waas mattur?'

Whan Young Wullie ded un ansur. Mawthur turnt ta Faathur, 'Boay's look en a bit whist.'

'Waas mattur?' Faathur ax'd es boay.

Young Wullie sid, 'Nawthen.' Ee anded Mawthur tha skool raa-port an scarppered up steers owt ov arms waay.

Mawthur rid tha skool raa-port, sha cum ovur weth a hot flush, an sat down braa queck. Whan sha waas feelun a bit fitty, sha sid, 'Faathur tha Tacher sez, Young Wullie es naw ambis-shun.'

'Giss on.' Faathur raa-pl'd, sarchen fer maa-ches en es trousies pawkuts.

Mawthur was git-un en a bit ov a flummex. 'Tis trew! Me poor dear chile, I shudn wender, twas es berth, cause ee cum fer ee waas due, an I bla-ame tha mid-wife, sha waas late. Tis pla-ane ta see, es effected tha boay.'

Faathur foun tha maa-ches, ee lit es rollie, aftur tha footh tempt, than ee scratch es ead thraw es cap afore ee sez, 'Geve tha fi-er a bit av a pauke, an putt tha kittle footh, yew need cuppa suggery tay, tis good fer shock missus.'

Mawthur ded az sha waas tolled, an wait'd, sha cud oall mos ear tha cogs turnun en Faathur's ead. Sha cuddn ang on fer Faathur ta fin'sh think-un, so sha blurted owt, 'Tha deear ob'm. Wat-evur ar wa gwain ta do?'

Faathur repl'd, 'Bless'd ef I knaw, wan thang fer sure, tha buoy daun't turn aftur mee, caus I cheeved oall mee ambis-shuns.'

'Onlay ambis-shun yew ad et skool waas gitten Mavis Tremayne b'hind tha bike sheds.' Mawthur snapped.

'Ere, ere,' Faathur push'd es cap back ferthur en es ead, ee alwuz ded thet whan ee waas gitten teasy. 'Naw point en raken tha up gain, I waas talkun bout propur ambis-shun, an I knaw I ded cheeve oall ob'm.'

'Wha ambis-shuns yew on bout?' Mawthur axed as sha maade tha tay.

'Proper skool ambis-shun missus.' Faathur took tha offured cup ef tay fer ee continued, 'I ad thray ambis-shuns, an I cheeved tham oall I ded.'

Mawthur waz plaised sha putt plen-taa ef suger en er tay, cause sha wa-as a bit afeerard ta ax'd. 'Yew aint tawld me woos tha ambisshuns tha yew haad et skool Faathur?'

Faathur smil't. 'Mee ambis-shuns waas ta drink beeer, smauke fags an ta sweer lik a troopur, an I'ab cheeved oall ob'm.'

# Back Ome Fram Lunnon

*Ride ta Lunnon un a hoss?*
*See wat monay et da coss.*
*Rub us raw and rub us bare*
*afore we da git alf-waay theere.*

Newlyn - November -1851

Liza Treneer waas owt ov breath fram run-nun, sha stopp'd en shout'd,
'Mary! Mary Kelynack!'

Liza ad bin coosun avtur a rid cloak'd, black hatt'd woman gwaine un
lik a long dog, en front ov ur, up tha nar-raw opewaay. Liza cudden bayleeve
tha woman, Mary Kelynack, waas eightay fower yer ole.

Mary Kelynack turn'd, look'd pass Liza owt ta sea, sha raised er walkun
stick an wav'd et en tha air. Fer a momunt Liza thawt Mary waas gwaine ta
showt, 'Hevva! - Hevva! an-noun-sun sha a spot'd a shoal ov pilchards.

En-sted weth a twinkle en ur eye Mary sid, 'Woss un Liza Treneer?
Naw-bod-daay wud stop theere hoss fram gal-lip-pun fer a maid thet caan't
caatch up weth en ole woman.'

Liza stramm'd up ta tha grizzlun octogenarain, paus'd, plac'd er ands
un ur hips en sid sternlay, 'Mary Kelynack, yew ole witch!'

Liza cud contane ur joy naw longur, sha thraw'd er arms roun tha oldur
woman, 'Oh Mary deare, I've bin saw wor-red bout yew, I've bin lik a hen
afore daay. Welcum ome.'

Tha toe friends walk'd, arm en arm, enta Mary's cottaage an hung theere
cloaks an ats un pegs bayhind tha spence dore.

'Geeve tha fi-er a poke an pull tha kittle forth.' Mary sid as sha settled
enta er cheer.

Liza smil'd. Sha ad a pot tay maade en naw time. Es soon es sha pour'd
tha tay, Liza ax'd, 'Mary yew nevur sid, bee nor baw ta me, wat paw-cess'd
yew ta do such a theng?'

Avtur a gaddle ov tay Mary ray-plied, 'Fore I telle, I'll saay tha saame
ta yew es I sid ta tha Mayuress ov Lunnon, ets a ansum cup tay.'

'Wat maade yew do et, waasn't ee feelun quite fitty en tha ed?'

'Et sound'd propur a new vang. I sid ta meself, Mary Kelynack, yew'r
gwaine ta the Grate Exhib-bis-shun ef et kills ee en tha ah-tempt.'

'But Mary ta walk ta Lunnon un yewr own! Ow long ded et taake?'

'Five wakes, et waas ard gwaine weth me cowel ovur me back, daay en,
daay owt, fer five wakes, sleepun en tha edge wen I ad ta.'

Tha concern shaw'd un Liza's faace, 'Mary waasn't yew wor-rid bowt yew knaw?'

'A chance wud aye bin a fine theng.' Mary Grezzled un add'd, 'Naw deare, ev-ray-bod-ee waas es gud es gold.'

'Wat waas et lik en Lunnon?'

'Wull Liza, thay waas ver-ray cut up en thay waay thay tawk'd, I cudden fathum en owt et furst, but I soon got tha ang obem.'

'Ded thay undur-stan yew Mary, cas thay es fer-enurs en Lunnon'

'Corse thay ded, tho sum-times I ad ta saay tha saame theng ovur agin, cos I da tawk awful broad. Like wen tha Mayur ax'd me wheer I waas fram, I thowt I wud maake et ee-saay fer un, saw I sid Lan's En, but ee dedent git et, saw I sid Penzance. Ee knawed thet wan.'

'Ow ded ee manaage fer monay?' Liza ax'd.

'Et tha truth be knawed Liza, I waas lik gwaine roun weth tha pla-ate en chapel, pick up a bit ere un a bit theere. Evun tha Mayur ov Lunnon, God bless un, geeve me a sov-run an ee ded-dun begritched et.'

'Tell me bout tha Grate Ex-hib-bis-shun?'

'Twas ansum, I wen down theere time n time agin, ta aye a gud geek oun, nevur seen nawthun lik et. Theere waas ovur a undred thousun differunt thengs. Lods ov new vangled gadgets, oall cost-tun a bra bit ov monay. My fay-rite waas the chris-taal fount-tun, et waas so purdaay, oall thet waatur shinun lik thousuns ov shoot-tun staars.'

Mary Kelynack sigh'd, fer a momunt sha waas back en Lunnon. Tha en-tur ov at-ten-shun. A Cornish charactur thet walk'd ta Lunnon ta see tha Grate Ex-hib-bis-shun an sha met...

'Mary. Mary yer miles awaay,' Liza sid kindlay, smilun et ur elderlay rony, 'Ded yew reallay mate tha Queen?'

Mary nodd'd, re-liv-un thet time agin.

'I ded Liza, ef I nevur shud move fram thus cheer agin, I ded. I waas ray-sent-tud ta ur Majestay Queen Vectoria an Prince Alburt un my laast isit ta tha Grate Ex-tlib-bis-shun.'

'Wat ded sha saay ta ee Mary? Wat ded Queen Vectoria saay ta ee?' Liza ax'd weth bat'd breath.

Mary Kelyneck luke'd down et er bent an twistud ands, sha felt tha pane v sore feet fram undreds of miles ov walkun. Sha raysed ur ed an weth a ear en ur eye luked et Liza.

'Tha Queen sid, wull dun Mary ets grate ta see yew ere.'

Tha sob raked tha frail ole body. Liza put er arms aroun Mary.

'Oh Mary deare, ev-ray wan en Newlyn es saw proud ov yew, doan't up-et yerselve. Yer ome now.'

# Buckshe

Tidden fitty ta do an act ov kindness an waant payun fer et. Henree Pascoe naw'd thus an ee wud alwaays do thengs buckshe fer anywan en tha villaage.

Henree? Yew naw Henree; tha son ov Lily Rawe that waas, yew naw Lily, sha's ben fowertay five fer dunkee's years. Iss, thet Lily Rawe! Tha wan... wull, sha's Lily Pascoe now. Iss, Lily Pascoe tha wan thet shines tha milk bottles weth windalean bevore sha puts em owt fer Percy tha milkman.

Anywaay nuff bout Lily Pascoe! Et's er boay Henree I waas gwain ta tellee bout. Tis common knowledge Henree does acts ov kindness fer peepull buckshe. Iss, buckshe! Henree does jobs fer peepull and ee doan't waant nuffun fer et.

Tis true. Othur daay, ee wen down shop fer Missus Kneebone and picked up a alf pound of clotted cream fer er, mind yew, sha cudden mind askun im ta do et.

Bayfore Missus Kneebone cud git er senses tagethur bout tha cream. Henree sid, 'Now I'm ere Missus Kneebone, I may es wull do a bit en tha garden fer ee. Corse, I'll do et buckshe.' An off ee went inta tha garden.

Wull, like theer waddun gwain ta be no tomorraw; Henree carring a gallun pail, en each, and waas back en Missus Kneebone's kitchun. 'Thet waas lucky Missus Kneebone,' Henree sid, weth a smile thet cud ave ben a advert fer Brasso, 'I just managed ta pick oall yew're strawberries bevore tha burds ate em.' Henree nodded an smilt agin, 'An I've pick'd um fer ee buckshe Missus Kneebone'.

'But Hen, Hen, Henree,' Missus Kneebone stuttered weth tha shock ov e oall. 'Wat am I gwain ta do weth galluns ov strawberries?'

'Wull twud be a shaame ta let em go ta waste.' Henree rayplied, 'I reckun tis faate yew askun me ta get thet cream fer ee.'

'Twud seem like et.' Missus Kneebone rayplied en an unsure voice, 'But cudden ate oall ov em strawberries, naw ow.'

'Telle wat I cud elp ee ate sum ov em... yew naw buckshe.'

'Wud ee do thet fer an ole wommen Henree'

'Iss, I wud. Tellee wat mind, rathur then let tham strawberries go ta waste. cos wull nevur ate um oall, not en a month ov Sundaays. Dreckly, I thenk yew shud maake strawberrie jaam weth tha wans thet's left...'

'Thas a gud idea Henree.'

'Iss tis, even ef I do saay et meself. An I tell ee wat rathur en ave tha jars o jaam wayun down tha shelf en tha kitchun I'll taake tha jam roun tha villag fer ee. Corse I'll do et buckshe and ef any wan was ta geeve me a trifle for th jam corse I'll share weth ee, twudden be faare else wud et.'

'Thas true Henree, very true...'

'Shull I pull tha kittle forth an maake nothur cup ov tay Missus Kneebone'.

# Oald Womman Et Orchard Cottage

Charlay Semmons stramm'd enta thay emptay kiddleywink. Ee wen strate up ta tha bar an gasp'd, 'Beer!' An wait'd weth es mouth abroad.

Tha pint waas ex-purt-lay pult. Tha lan-lurd knaw'd es stuff, ee waas ome fram ome, real propur et es job.

Charlay Semmens, must ave bin es dry es oald boots, ee gaddled alf ov es pint es soon es ee got et. Wip'd es mouth un es sleeve, 'Wat do ee knaw bout thet oald womman thet lives, en tha cottage, gwaine owt ov tha village tawurds Trura?' Ee ax'd es ost.

'Do ee mane tha oald womman thet lives en Orchard Cottage?' Bill Kemp, lan-lurd ov tha kiddley wink, answur'd by waay ov nothur quest-un ta es onlay custmur.

'Iss, iss thas tha wan. I feel I knaw er, but I caan't caall er ome.' Charlay rayplied, tryun ta sound a bit vague.

'Queer ole devil.'

'Sha es.' Charlay emptud es glass, un push et towards tha lan-lurd.

'Saame agin?' Bill Kemp ax'd.

'Iss, Iss. Saame agin, I need et.' Charlay rayplied.

'Thay saay sha's a witch!' Bill sid, as ee put tha pint down, un tha bar, en front ov es customur.

Charlay gasp'd, tuke nothur gaddle, wip'd es mouth agin, an sid en a voice thet didn't seem fitty. 'Giss on?'

'Tis true.' Bill Kemp nodd'd and raypeat'd, 'Tis true.'

'A witch.' Charlay sid ta es-self, an ran es fingers threw es theck crop ov black hair, ee luked et es hand, turn'd et ovur. Wen ee saw Bill Kemp ukun et em ee grizzled, 'A witch.'

'Thas rite.'

'Giss on!' Charlay sid, wishun ee never ax'd.

Bill Kemp waas warmun ta tha subject. 'Iss, iss, sha es,' ee continu'd en a con-fid-ent-shall whisper, 'ded ee see tha toads en er gardun, geat lickurs, en tha ole womman got umteen caats, oall black wans. Naw wandur, thay aay sha's a witch.'

'Naw thas ole wives taales,' Charlay stat'd, thow et mus bay sid ee gone shaade whitur. 'Thet's naw proof.' Ee add'd ta convince esself.

'Sha maakes love po-shuns!' Bill emphasized es point.

'Cod's wallop thet es.'

'I wudden bay ta sure, we've nevur ad a divorce en tha village.'

'Naw. Doan't reckun yew caan put ta much un thet wan. Thet's wat they caall cir-cum-stan-shall.' Charlay ray-sun'd, indee-cate-un ee wantud nothur pint.

Bill Kemp pick'd up tha emptay glass an eld et en front ov Charlay's faace. 'Notice sum theng, do ee?'

'Unlay me emptay glass.'

'Luke et me fingurs!'

'Yer nales es lagg'd,' Charlay grizzl'd. 'Taint propur.'

'Not me nales, me fingurs, naw warts, ad loads ov warts las week I ded. Tha oald womman fram Orchard Cottage charm'd em ov.' Bill Kemp pult tha pint. 'Tha's tha God's onest trewth thet es, sha ded charm em.' Ee nodd'd. 'Sha caan geeve tha evil eye as-wull so thay saay!'

Charlay stared et tha pint. Ee luked like deth warm'd up. Ee ran es fingurs threw es hair agin and then stud'd es hand turnun et ovur an ovur.

'Whiskay, maake et a doub-bull.'

Bill Kemp knawd wen ta kape quiet, ee waas tha perfict lan-lurd. Ee gaave tha glass two gental pushes et tha optic, eld tha glass up ta tha lite, shook es head, an gaave tha optic a queck push ta release nothur drop en ta tha whiskay glass. Ee plaac'd tha glass en front ov Charlay. 'I oall-waays geeve gud measure un a doub-bull.' Ee sid, nod-dun et tha glass.

Et waas ob-vious-lay appre-sha-atud by Charlay, ee down'd et en wan gaddle. Ran es fingurs threw es hair agin an gasp'd. Ee stud up quecklay.

'Sha sid me hair wud fall owt!' He blurt'd, showun Bill Kemp a handful ov loose hair.

Tha lan-lurd ray-fill'd tha whiskay glass weth a doub-bull an add'd two drops more fer gud measure. 'Wat ded ee do?' Bill Kemp ax'd.

Charlay Semmens down'd tha whiskay. 'Run ovur wan over bloody caats. Kilt et ded.' Ee put tha glass down an turn'd es hands ovur. 'Luke hair es growun un me hans now!' Ee exclaim'd.

# Wan Fer Sarraw

Mavis Caddy ad ben tha poast-womman, en tha Cornish village ov Penkie, fer twen-nee yers. Mavis ad daay-liver'd tha poast ta tha village en-habet-tants, owt-lie-yun farms un cot-tages, en oall-sorts ov weth-hur. Proud-lay ad-mit-tun sha ad nevur miss'd a daay's wurk en er life.

Oall-tho et waas mid Septembur, et waas ansum weth-hur. Mavis waas stull wearun er sumhur isshue poast ovvuss u-ne-form. Tha sun ad shone oall mornun, sha ad oall-moast finush'd er un foot daay-liver-rays an' dedn't feel tired.

Walkun down tha countray rawd ta, Orchard Cottage, tha laast daay-liver-ray un er roun. Mavis nawticed tha bram-bull strewn hedges waas chuck a block weth black-berras. Sha maade up er mind ta cum back latur, en tha av-noon, ta pick em.

Tha Munroe famlay mov'd ta Orchard Cottage thray months ago. Mavis wen ta theer ouse wance a month ta daay-liver, tha onlay mail thay evur ray-ceiv'd, tha cell-o-faane wrapp'd, 'Gun Magazine.'

Mavis lift'd tha lettur box flaap ta be great'd by a rays'd female voice, 'I'm fed up weth yew, an yewr gun mania, et's me or tha guns!'

Wat-evur else waas sid wen unhurd; tha Gun Magazine fell ta tha floor, tha spring back lettur box flaap snapp'd shut.

Mavis walk'd awaay won-dur-un ef tha hand gun law waas beun ignor'd. Sha day-sided et waas nun over buznezz. Mavis claws'd tha gerden gaate an nawticed a sol-lit-tary magpie sittun un tha fence.

'Wan fer sarraw,' Mavis sid, spit-tun en tha rawd ta ward ovv bad luck.

*****

Jean Monroe lay un tha bed, sha breath'd en deep-lay. 'Count ta tin', sha told erself. Feelun calmur sha start'd ta thenk lod-gical-lay, bout er usband, Bill's obbay ov col-lect-tun hand guns.

Oall men need-ded a obbay. Thus waas moore then a obbay. Et waas un ob-sess-shun. Sence thay ad moved, ta Orchard Cottage, Bill ad ellegally purchaas'd nothur thray hand guns fram othur collecturs givun up tha obbay aftur tha tragic Dunblane massacre.

Bill clean'd, load'd an unload'd tha guns um-teen times a daay. Ee waas con-stant-lay watch'd by, Joey, theer sebben yer oald son. Joey waas daggun ta fi-er tha guns. Ee kept askun es faathur ef ee cud old tha guns an fi-er em.

Bill waas ovur tha moon weth es boay's entur-rust. En fairnuss, Bill waas oall-waays careful, Joey onlay handl'd unload'd guns. Bill emfa-sis'd load'd guns waas dan-ger-us.

Uz a mawthur, Jean, believ'd er son onlay associat'd dan-ger-rus weth cross-sun tha rawd wethowt lookun. Sha waas afeer'd, wan daay, an ax-ced-dent wud appun.

Uz a wife, Jean felt sha waas balanc'd un a knife edge, tha rows baytween er an Bill bout tha guns were be-cumun moore reglar. Tha row thet mornun ad ben bout a gun left un tha dinun room taybull tha nite avore, thenk-ful-lay unload'd. Sha ad foun young Joey play-un weth tha gun wen sha ad taken en es brek-fass.

Jean mede-ate-lay flew unta a raage an con-front'd Bill bout be-un careless. Ee laff'd an sid sha waas ovur re-act-tun, thet waas wen sha threatun ta leb im. Bill dedn't answur, ee jus wen ta collect tha poast ee ad eard beun day-liver'd.

Bill waas flippun thraw tha latest, 'Gun Magazine', wen ee cum back enta tha room. Jean rush'd owt ov tha room, slamm'd tha door an stank'd upsteers.

Aving finish'd er dut-tays, fer tha village poast ovvus, Mavis wen ome. Sha chang'd owt over uni-e-form enta cas-u-oall jeans and sweatur.

Mavis ad a jammy maw an a cup ov tay, fer er crouse. Soon uz sha ad fenesh'd, sha slipp'd un er walkun shoes an a oald poast ovvus beret ta protect er ead fram ovur angun bram-bulls. Suit-ab-lay attired, an arm'd weth a large jug, sha set ovv ta pick tha black-berrus sha ad seen er-la-ur.

Mavis walk'd ta tha laane, leadun ta Orchard Cottage, an start'd ta pick tha moast suc-u-lent black-berrus sha ad evur seen. I've timed thus rite sha thaw't, tha black-berrus wur so ripe, thay fell enta er and wen sha touch'd tham. Mavis oallso knaw'd sha waas pickun obem avore tha 29th of Septembur, wen accordun ta folklore, tha debbel wud spoil tha blackberrus makun tham unsafe ta ate.

Mavis ten-shun ta tha black-berrus waas entur-rupt-tud by a loud raucous caall, tha magpie waas sittun un tha branch ov a nearby tray, Mavis doff'd er beret en salute, nother waay ov wardun ov bad luck.

'Ovv weth yew, me black n white friend.' Sha sid.

Mavis laffed, tha magpie flew awaay. Me an my sup-per-sti-shuns sha thaw't, ray-turn-un ta tha job en and. Tha ovv dutay poast wom-mem sang, en a skule plaaygroun chant, 'Wan fer sarraw...'

Jean woke up, weth a start, an look'd et tha bedroom clock. Et waas 1.30 en tha avnoon, sha ad ben asleep fer two ours. Sha felt guilty an rush'd downsteers.

Er boay, Joey, waas sittiun et tha tay-bull loadun live am-u-nis-shun enta a lethal lookun pistol.

'Joey! Put thet gun down et once. Et's dan-ger-rus!' Jean xclaim'd.

Tha sebben yer oald jump'd, 'I'm not do-un nawthun wrong Mawthur.' Ee whimper'd, uz ee slid tha gun awaay.

'Go owt enta tha gerden an plaay thus min-nit!' Es mawthur snapped, 'I want a wurd weth yewr faathur un es own.'

Joey ran owt threw tha patio doors, weth-owt a back-ward glance. Bill cum stridun enta tha room an demand'd, 'Woss oall tha row bout, et souns like Lansan jail.'

Fer a momunt Jean waas et a loss fer wurds. En angur sha took er weddun ring ow an threw et un tha table beside tha a-band-un pistol.

Jean took a deep breath, look'd et er uzband an sid en a calm voice. 'Thet es et, I'm takun Joey ta mawthurs. Tha mar-rage es ovur!'

Sha rush'd upsteers ta pack follow'd by er uzband protestun et er re-act-shun, avore ee start'd pleadun weth er ta staay.

Joey hid-un behin tha Cornish Palm en tha gerden saw an ovurhurd everay-theng. Ee waas won-dur-un wat ta do, wen tha ouse went silent. Mawthur an Faathur wud be do-un thet sop-pay kissun an makun up, ee reckun'd, run-nun ta plaay un tha swing.

Joey waas swingun highur then ee ad evur dun avore, wen ee saw tha magpie land en tha gardun. Ee slow'd tha swing down by lettun es feet drag un tha groun', es mind raaced tin ta tha dozen.

Magpie, wan fer sarraw. Magpies liked shiny teengs. Mawthur's weddun ring waas shiny. Wan fer sarraw. Joey ran enta tha ouse.

Disturb'd by Joey tha magpie flew an perch'd un tha gerden gaate, flick'd ets tail an geeved a teasy soundun caall. Joey ran back enta tha gerden clutch-un tha pistol. Ee stead'd emself, aim'd an fi-er'd et tha magpie. Tha recoil ov tha pistol scat Joey ta tha groun. Tha magpie screech'd an flew awaay.

Tha bedroom windaw waas throw'd abroad. Bill n Jean shout'd en horror. 'Joey put tha gun dohwn et's dan-ger-rus!'

Tha magpie foun' a saafe pia ace ta perch an look'd et Mavis.

'Wan fer sorraw.' Mavis moan'd. Sha waas es white es a goast, n clutchun tha bleedun wound en er leg. 'I'm gwaine ta miss wurk fer tha furst time tamorraw.' Mavis sid, bay-fower sha paas'd owt weth tha pain.

# Missus Laity's Tay Room

Missus Laity decided ta cash en on tha visitur buznuzz fram er cottage on tha St Ives rawd. Sha dedden wan ta bothur weth bed-n-brekfas, so sha opun'd a tayroom, twas decked owt weth flew-wurs an sha used er bess cloam. Tha menu waas writ un a blackbord weth a bet ov chaalk er granson gived er.

Missus Laity ded knaw wat visiturs liked, sha ad creem tays, saffern caake, plus a load ov nicey an twas oall ome maade.

Decky Bray tha odd job man waas passun Missus Laity's plaace so ee thaw'd ee wud ave a geek an geeve er bit ov custom. Ee wen inta tha tayroom, an sed, 'I'll ave cup tay, Missus Laity ef yew plaise.'

Missus Laity waas glad ta see Decky, fact waas ee waas er furst custmer but sha dedden tell Decky that. Sha give tha fi-er a bit ov a pauke an pult tha kittle forth, sha ad fresh tay maade en nixt ta naw time.

Wen Missus Laity gave Decky es cup ov tay. Decky sed, 'I oall waays pay cash Missus Laity, ow much do I owe ee?'

'Thas sixpence,' Missus Laity ray-plied.

Decky countud owt six pennes fram tha coins en es and an geve et ta Missus Laity. 'I ebbem got much mon-nay,' Decky sed, 'but, ow much es yer cheepest bit ov sum theng ta ate?'

Missus Laity knawing Decky cudden read or rite wen thraw tha menu tellun em tha prices.

'Tis naw good,' Decky sed wen sha ad finished readden obem owt. 'I caan't ford nun ov em, 'ow much es et fer a bit ov bred n buttur?'

'Fower pence.' Missus Laity sed, sha waas gitten bit fed up weth Decky by thus time, but tha custmer es alwaays rite sha tole ersell.

'Ow much es a bit ov bred n marjareen?' Decky ax'd.

'Thray pence.' Missus Laity ansured.

Decky queek-lay took a geek et es mon-nay, 'Naw good, I gotta git baccy es well, ow much es a bit ov bred weth-owt buttur?'

'Tuppence, surly yew caan ford that Decky?' Missus Laity ax'd, begunning ta feel a bit teasy weth Decky.

'Naw tain't es simpall es thet,' Decky sed. 'I gotta lot on thus week. Ef a bit ov bred weth-owt buttur es tuppenee, ow much es a bit ov bred weth-owt marjareen mus be cheeper?'

'Corse tis yew ejit, thas onlay a penny.'

Decky smilt, 'Now yer talkun, I'll ave a bit ov bred weth owt marjareen.'

# Arfurr

Ee wuz fo-wur fut nuthun,
eed go ta a do un sey,
'Who wuz tha tallust bloke
furr I cum un.'

Ee cud thraw
a shapt six ench nale
un tha treb-bul twen-nee
uftur drinkun a gallun ov slops.

Back long twuz oall tha ra-age
furr Arfurr ta ate flew-wurs
graw-un longside tha rawd
furr es crouse.

Ee evun swal-lad a worm
furr devil-ment, aftur ee sud,
'Tha worm ee cum owt
ell ov alot biggur yew.'

Teday Arfurr uz en es coffun
wid tha lid nailt tight.
Tis decked owt wid flew-wurs
dreckly tha'll git eaved un tha tip.

Tiz pla-ane ta see,
en nixt ta naw time,
tha worms uz goin
ta git tha awn back un Arfurr.

# Tha Ra-un-yun

Jonnay Fortnite
Where ave ee bin?

> Cross tha pond.

Ell ov a jaunt.
Sell mutch ded ee?

> Naw, ef ee must knaw,
> I took up anothur job.

Wat ded ee do?

> Set up un me awn
> tappun boots.

Iss iss, gud traade spect yew
maade a trifle weth thet wan.

> Naw. Not a lot ov caall
> fer et yew.

Wot do ee mane?

> Wull see, thay party,
> Rid Inyans they waas caalt
> went barefut, twudden fitty.

Giss un.

> Tis true
> I served me-selve sum arm,
> I was penny liggan,
> ad ta work me passaage ome.

Well tis gud ta see ee agin,
cummes en, ave a bit of croust,
an a touch pipe. Less see ef we caan
schemey rathur un lowster.

# Tha Waay

Aftur los-un tha,
'I doant-wun-ta go,' rowteen.
Ee wus subjek-tad ta,
'Yo'll graw inta em trousies.'
An, 'Don git tha white shart dabbered.'
Weth Faathur's tie knot-ted tween,
'Yer strang-glun mee.'
An, 'Yo gotta luke smert.'

Ee wen ta Sundee Sko-ool
weth Shal-lah, (sha ad teeff braa-ses)
thro owt tha sarvice, thay loff'd, gig-gled
an pult faa-ses.

Whan thay wuz traapsin ome
Shal-lah tache-em
tha waay
grawn-ups kesse.

Aftur, ovar tay
ween slurp an sip
nawthur ax'd em,
Doss ee knaw ef ee wuz goin agin.'

I'm daggin ta go nixt Sundee,
f I'm dress'd fitty,
in I ave joey fer God's pla- ate
em az Shal-lah.'
ie ra-pl'd, lick-un es brewsed lip.

# Tha Bals Aar Knack'd

Gone aar tha daays
ov adventurers
avun shares an doles ov tin.

Naw gud prospecting now,
seams arn't follow'd naw more
lodes aar ta be left weth en.

Gunnis aar tha scals
belongun ta learys now
theers not a skove ta keep.

Tha kibble's scat,
launders smashed ta smithereens
an tha stulls aar burred deep.

Dags aar blunt,
ammers aar dun cobbing
an tha whims arn't makin a sound.

Tulls es en museums,
touch pipes and crowst
aar memories underground.

Gud bye ta trunking,
tribute daays aar ovur
tha miner's dun es last core.

Grass es naw greener,
an tha blawin house
es hungary fer ore.

Tha bals aar knack'd
an tis a cirtain shame
Cornish minun es naw more.

# Waon't Tell a Sawl

Decky Bray tha odd job man
iz got a windaw cleanun roun
ram midnite til fower n tha mornun.

> I waon't tell a sawl,
> thou I mus saay ee's lookun wisht.

knaw thet. I urd es gwaine weth
ha widow wemman, yew knaw
ha wan thet wears oall thet maake-up.

> I knaw zackly who yew mane
> muttun dress'd uz lamb, I saay.

hay saay er laast uzban ax-sid-ent-lay
ied fram aten poisun mushrooms
n tha wan bayfower ee fell down tha well.

> Giss on weth ee,
> wat evur es tha wurld cummun ta.

es true, an tidden tha furst time
Decky Bray es stray'd fram ome.
ack long, ee wen fishun fer a month.

> Deary me, an ees missus is church gwaine
> sha wudden saay boo ta a goose

Nearur my God ta thee, sha sid ta me
hus mornun. Aftur sha stay'd tha nite
ursun tha parson, ef yew knaw wat I mean.

> I do mae dear, I do,
> an ee shud naw bettur en es job.

ss ee shud. Yew knaw nutthun
vur appens roun ere, ef et ded,
awbody wud talk bout et.

> Tha's true tain't thet sort ov a plaace.
> Mus git on, see ef mae naybers ome.

# Uz Thay Saay

Onest uz tha daay es long,
Esme jis caan't raysist taaken ome
oall tha complay-mentray paakets
ov sugur, saalt, peppur, saauces
left fur custmur conven-yance.

Strate uz a die,
Esme who oall-waays seems ta find
lost pursus, walluts,
oall sorts ov pens n pencils.
Nevur manages ta find tha ownhurs
findurs keepurs uz thay saay.

Gud uz gold,
Esme who elps char-it-tay
weth fund raysun, coffay mornuns,
jumbull saales an bring n buy stoalls.
Keepun a lit-till back ta covur xpensus.

Litnun tha loaad,
Esme who elps oall tha penshunners,
seck n desabull'd weth theere shop-pun
nevur quite avun nuff chaange
ta geve em wen tha job es dun.

Waittun fur er boat ta cum en
Esme who bayleeves tha Lord
elps tham thet elps thamselves.

# Gud News

Mygar,
tha wind blaw'd
em en. Thray obem.
Doan't saay bee or bow.

Chuffs,
stoall theer nest
fram ovur tha watur.
Doan't tull a saul.

Propur,
makun tha moast
obem cummun ome.
Kape et ta yerself.

Ansum,
ien's clucky,
sittun es tight es a dam.
Saay nuthun.

Ell-up,
sum party tri'd
a shrub tha nest.
Doan't coose bout et.

Purdy,
tha eggs es bealed
Arfurr es back.
Tull tha werld!

# Gwain Quietlay

Fine wurds doan't buttur parsnips:
en sha waas jes lik Lady Fan Todd
dress'd ta death en kill'd weth fashun.

Now, ee lik ta gwain quietlay.
But, oppertunitay es a bit lik eggs;
thay cum wan et a time... Ee shouted,
'Yewr dress'd up lik a oss mareen!'

Er faace went rid es beetroot, en er mouth
screw'd up lik a duck's fert. She draw'd
ersell up, full wate wethowt tha wrappur.
'En yewr nawthun but a geet booba.'

Es yew naw ee lik'd ta gwain quietlay,
but, ee cudden laive thet wan go.
'Eny waay I doan't fooch awaay time
geekun owt ov windas oall daay.'

Et waas a rid rag ta a bull,
'I supose I shud speck thet
fram a lemb ov tha debil - nathun lik
tha pot callun tha kittle black.'

Wull ee wantud ta gwain quietlay
en sha waas gittun es dander up,
ee naw'd ee ad ta bite es tongue.
'Ets time fer me ta buckle to en git dun.'

Sha realised ee waas offerun a waay owt
'I'm feelun no how, not lik me tall, s'pose
I da luke lik muttun dress'd up es lamb.'

'Naw, not et oall,' ee ray-plied n shook es ead,
'I thenk yewr lukun propur. En tha fashion
es thay saay - nathun lik a bit ov fal de rals.'

'Do ee thenk so?'

'Iss, but doan't let et go ta yewr ead mind -
jus gwain quietlay.'

# Dislexic Dialectisshun

Tawk bout endullgents...
hus poem es wan ov tha long intra-duck-shuns wat es en tha fashun...

Thus concerns tha emportance of letturs, souns an ab-brev-e-ashuns,
en Cornish poetray thet ave spashal con-she-quences
ur a dislexic dialectisshun. And now the poem...

Dvur Porkellis A is cut
en card en putt en an A rick.
Down St Ives thers a H en artist
en I does naw E es a Cornishman.

En Trura Skool
RE es acceptabull mythoalagee
wheer evun dislexics
ann bayleeve en God es long
es et starts weth a capital D
en I does naw E es a Cornishman.

If yew waant ta ear a locaal P
go ovur ta Camburn Gents,
wheer thay caall eache othur pard
en I does naw E es a Cornishman.

Now, I'll tellee bout Les Merton;
en I does naw E es a Cornishman
en E wull do es best ta assure yew
theers an F en Phoenix en Ridruth.

## *Glossary*

Please note: the glossary explanations of Kernewek and Cornish dialect words refer to the words used in this book, the same Cornish dialect word may also have another meaning if used in another context.

| | |
|---|---|
| abroad | open |
| adventurers | those that have shares in a mine |
| avore | before |
| ax'd | asked |
| bal | mine |
| bayleeve | believe |
| bealed | egg cracked by bird hatching |
| Benny | Joker, highest value card |
| bevore | before |
| begritcht | begrudge |
| bra | lot, plenty, |
| booba | fool |
| buckler | circular wooden cover |
| buckshe | free |
| Camburn | Camborne |
| chacks | cheeks |
| cheeved | achieved |
| clucky | broody |
| cabing | snatching fish from passing gurries |
| card | carried |
| cowl rooz | cast the net. |
| cobbing | breaking the ore with hammers |
| coosun | chasing, pursuing |
| core | mining term for shifts |
| cowel | fish basket |
| crouse | snack, meal |
| cudden | could not |
| chuffs | Cornish chough a member of the crow family |
| cut up | posh |
| dabbered | dirty |
| debbel | devil |
| dags | axes |
| dreckly | later |
| dunkees | donkeys |
| edge | hedge |
| eightay | eighty |
| emmets | visitors, tourists |
| euchred | a method of beating euchre card opponents |
| eaved | thrown |
| faathur | father |

| | |
|---|---|
| athum | understand |
| ier | fire |
| itty | well, proper |
| lew-wers | flowers |
| lummex | bewildered state |
| ower | four |
| addle | to drink quickly |
| eat | great |
| eek | look |
| in | steel jawed animal trap |
| rizzlun | grinning |
| ud | good |
| urries | hand carts |
| waine | going |
| evva | shout to announce a shoal of pilchards |
| uer | lookout |
| ss | yes |
| onnay Fortnitc | packman, pedlar |
| esse | kiss |
| ibble | an iron bucket that goes up and down in a mine shaft |
| iddleywink | pub, house selling alcohol |
| ittle | kettle |
| agg'd | dirty |
| ansen | Launceston |
| aunders | gutters used for the conveyance of water |
| earys | remains of old mine and stream workings |
| emb | limb |
| ong dog | greyhound |
| owster | manual work |
| iked | looked |
| unnon | London |
| awthur | mother |
| ythoalagee | mythology |
| icey | sweets |
| bem | of them |
| le | old |
| la-ate | plate |
| enny liggan | short of money |
| laise | please |
| oast | post |
| urdaay | pretty |
| awkut | pocket |
| inny | apron |
| awd | road |
| aw fry | a mainly potato meal |
| idruth | Redruth |

| | |
|---|---|
| rollies | hand made cigarettes |
| seams | lodes |
| scals | sections of ground |
| scat | broken |
| skool | school |
| smauke | smoke |
| smithereens | bits, tiny pieces |
| sov-run | sovereign |
| spence | cupboard under the stairs |
| shrub | rob, steal |
| stem | moored area for fishing boat |
| strammed | walked with a purpose |
| stulls | support timber in a mine |
| tawk'd | talked |
| tay | tea |
| teasy | angry, annoyed |
| thray | three |
| tidden | it isn't |
| touch pipe | smoke |
| trapsed | walked |
| tribute | pay according to ore raised |
| trousies | trousers |
| tucking | lifting the fish out of the sea in baskets |
| tulls | miner's helmet |
| un | on |
| vang | idea, notion |
| wakes | weeks |
| whims | machines for raising ore worked by steam, horse or water |
| whist | poorly |
| woss | what's |
| wraslar | wrestler |
| yer | year |
| zackly | exactly |

# Awards

*Arthur*
Won the Gorseth Kernow Dialect Verse competition 1998
*Tha Waay*
Won the Gorseth Kernow Dialect Verse competition 1999
*Ambis-shun*
Was awarded second place in Gorseth Kernow Dialect Prose competition 1999
*Uz Thay Saay*
Won the Gorseth Kernow Dialect Verse competition 2000
*Outhouse*
A Forward Press shortlisted poem in the Top 100 Poets 2000
*I Waon't Tell A Sawl*
Won the Gorseth Kernow Dialect Verse competition in 2001
*A Miner's Tale*
Won the Esethvos Kernow Competition for the best English Short Story 2001
*Palores*
Was awarded second place in Gorseth Kernow Short Story competition 2001
*Wan Fur Saaraw*
Was awarded third place in Gorseth Kernow Dialect Prose competition 2001
*Tha Ra-un-yun*
Was awarded second prize Dehwelans Dialect Poetry competition 2002
*Back Ome Fram Lunnun*
Won the Dehwelans Dialect Prose competition 2002
*Gud News*
Won the Gorseth Kernow Dialect Verse competition in 2002
*Tha Oald Womman Et Orchard Cottage*
Was awarded third place in Gorseth Kernow Dialect Prose competition 2002
*In the Presence of a Standing Stone*
Adult Runner Up Truro Ottakar's & Faber Poetry Competition 2002
*Fish into Rock*
Adult Runner Up Truro Ottakar's & Faber Poetry Competition 2003
*Gwain Quietlay*
Was awarded third place in Gorseth Kernow Dialect Verse competition 2004
*The Bals Aar Knack'd*
Was awarded second prize in Gorseth Kernow Dialect Verse competition 2006
*Buckshe*
Gained a highly commended place in Gorseth Kernow Dialect Prose competition 2006

# Also by Les Merton:

*Cornish Dialect*
Missus Laity's Tay Room
Oall Rite Me Ansum

*Cornish Noir*
Dark Corners

*Cornish Humour*
The Official Encyclopaedia of the Cornish Pasty

*Cornish Wildlife*
The Spirit of a King
Adders in Cornwall the facts, folklore and literature

*Poetry*
Cornflakes and Toast
Light the Muse
As Yesterday Begins
Inspired by Outlaws

*As Editor*
101 Poets for a Cornish Assembly